ALTERNATOR BOOKS™

MAE JEMISON

TRAILBLAZING ASTRONAUT

HEATHER E. SCHWARTZ

Lerner Publications ◆ Minneapolis

Lerner Publications Company
An imprint of Lerner Publishing Group, Inc.
241 First Avenue North
Minneapolis, MN 55401 USA

For reading levels and more information, look up this title at www.lernerbooks.com.

Main body text set in Aptifer Sans LT Pro.
Typeface provided by Linotype AG.

Editor: Brianna Kaiser

Library of Congress Cataloging-in-Publication Data

Names: Schwartz, Heather E., author.
Title: Mae Jemison : trailblazing astronaut / by Heather E. Schwartz.
Description: Minneapolis, MN : Lerner Publications, [2022] | Series: Boss lady bios (Alternator Books) | Includes bibliographical references and index. | Audience: Ages 8–12 | Audience: Grades 4–6 | Summary: "Mae Jemison, the first Black woman in space, is an engineer, physician, teacher, Peace Corps volunteer, and founder of multiple technology companies. This fascinating bio tells about her inspiring story on Earth and beyond"— Provided by publisher.
Identifiers: LCCN 2020021733 (print) | LCCN 2020021734 (ebook) | ISBN 9781728404561 (library binding) | ISBN 9781728417660 (ebook)
Subjects: LCSH: Jemison, Mae, 1956—Juvenile literature. | African American women astronauts—Biography—Juvenile literature. | Women astronauts—United States—Biography—Juvenile literature. | Astronauts—United States—Biography—Juvenile literature. | Manned space flight—Juvenile literature.
Classification: LCC TL789.85.J46 S39 2022 (print) | LCC TL789.85.J46 (ebook) | DDC 629.450092 [B]—dc23

LC record available at https://lccn.loc.gov/2020021733
LC ebook record available at https://lccn.loc.gov/2020021734

Manufactured in the United States of America
2-1008942-49028-9/27/2022

TABLE OF CONTENTS

Jemison aboard the *Endeavour* shuttle in 1992

REACHING HER DREAM

IN SEPTEMBER 1992 MAE JEMISON WAS HIGH ABOVE EARTH, TRAVELING THROUGH SPACE ON THE *ENDEAVOUR* SHUTTLE. She could see more stars than she'd ever seen before. Being in space made her see everything in a whole new way. She recognized that Earth was a part of the universe. She felt herself as part of the universe too, just like a star or a comet.

Jemison remembered herself as a young girl who dreamed of going into space. How excited she would have been to reach this lifelong dream! Jemison has reflected on this moment later in her life. "I thought about the little girl who assumed she would go into space. What would my younger self have thought if she met me? And I think she would have been tickled," she said.

Jemison was one of seven crew members to launch into space aboard the *Endeavour*.

Jemison grew up in Chicago, Illinois.

CHAPTER 1 GROWING UP

MAE CAROL JEMISON WAS BORN IN DECATUR, ALABAMA, ON OCTOBER 17, 1956. She moved to Chicago when she was three. She lived there with her parents, Charlie and Dorothy Jemison, and her two older siblings, Ada and Charles. Her mother was an elementary school teacher, and her father was a roofer and carpenter.

Mae loved dance as a child. Here, two professional dancers display their talent.

From an early age, Mae loved science and dance. She was excited to learn about the world and always wanted to know more. When she wasn't dancing or exploring the outdoors, her uncle taught her about science. Her parents supported her interest in science and encouraged her to always ask questions.

Mae wanted to become a scientist one day. But during the 1950s and 1960s, Black girls weren't expected to be scientists when they grew up. In kindergarten, Mae's teacher encouraged her to be a nurse instead of a scientist. Clear obstacles stood in the way of her dreams, but she held onto them anyway.

"WHAT DO YOU DO WITH THE OBSTACLES THAT PEOPLE PUT IN FRONT OF YOU? YOU CAN BUY INTO THEM, OR YOU CAN GIVE THE OBSTACLES BACK TO THAT PERSON."

Nichelle Nichols played Lieutenant Nyota Uhura on *Star Trek*.

Mae became particularly interested in space and dreamed of traveling there. She found inspiration on the TV show *Star Trek*. Lieutenant Nyota Uhura, played by actress Nichelle Nichols, was a strong Black woman working in space. She became a role model for Mae.

Mae grew up watching the Apollo moon missions on TV. She noticed none of the astronauts were women.

The crew of the first Apollo spaceflight did not include any women or people of color.

It didn't make sense to her. "I was really irritated that there were no women astronauts and there were no people of color," she said. "I thought, *What about if aliens run into this crew? They're going to think that those are the only people on Earth.* I thought it was unreasonable not to have everyone represented."

Mae continued studying both dance and science, and by the time she got to high school, she'd decided she wanted to be a biomedical engineer. This would allow her to focus on building equipment to solve medical problems. She was a hardworking student and earned a scholarship to Stanford University in California. She went there after graduating from high school in 1973.

In 1992 Jemison (*right*) attends a ceremony at Morgan Park High School. She graduated from the school in 1973.

GETTING IT DONE!

Mae graduated from high school and started attending Stanford at the age of sixteen.

Jemison studied chemical engineering at Stanford.

CHAPTER 2
GETTING TO WORK

SINCE STANFORD DIDN'T HAVE A PROGRAM IN BIOMEDICAL ENGINEERING, SHE STUDIED CHEMICAL ENGINEERING INSTEAD. One summer during college, Jemison got sick and saw a doctor who encouraged her to pursue a medical degree. A professor agreed. It made sense to her that learning more about medicine and the human body would be useful if she wanted to engineer medical equipment.

"You can't just build this little piece of equipment, and then not figure out whether it's going to be useful to a person. Will the person actually use it? How is it going to change their lifestyle? So being in medicine was going to be very important," she said.

Jemison (*right*) attends Stanford's 1996 graduation ceremony.

Jemison, who went to Stanford, gives a speech to Stanford's 1996 graduating class.

Jemison graduated from Stanford in 1977 with a bachelor of science in chemical engineering and a bachelor of arts in African American studies. Then she began medical school at Cornell University, and she studied dance at the Alvin Ailey American Dance Theater. While still a student, she volunteered in Cuba and Kenya, as well as at a Cambodian refugee camp in Thailand.

After earning her doctorate in medicine in 1981, Jemison worked as a general practitioner and also volunteered for the Peace Corps. By 1983 she was the Peace Corps medical officer for Sierra Leone and Liberia. She would later say being a Peace Corps doctor was the toughest job she ever had.

"I WAS ON CALL SEVEN DAYS A WEEK, 24 HOURS A DAY, 365 DAYS A YEAR, AND I WAS RESPONSIBLE FOR PEOPLE'S LIVES AND THEIR HEALTH. I WAS THE PERSON THAT WAS THERE. PERIOD."

In the Peace Corps, volunteers are sent to help people in other countries. Here, volunteers teach farming practices in West Africa.

After leaving the Peace Corps, Jemison returned to her work as a general practitioner. Although she had several degrees and a great deal of experience, she didn't feel she was finished learning. She started taking graduate classes in engineering. She also looked into her childhood dream of traveling into space.

By then her odds of reaching that goal had improved. Sally Ride had become the first American woman to go into space in 1983. If Ride could do it, Jemison was sure she could do it too. In 1985 Jemison applied to the National Aeronautics and Space Administration (NASA) astronaut program.

Sally Ride paved the way for other American women to go into space.

Engine exhaust fills the sky after the *Challenger* exploded on January 28, 1986.

CHAPTER 3

LIVING HER DREAM

JEMISON'S TIMING WAS OFF. In January 1986 the space shuttle *Challenger* exploded. It was a major disaster, and NASA temporarily stopped accepting new applicants to its astronaut program. She applied again in 1987, along with more than two thousand other applicants. Jemison was one of only fifteen chosen for the program.

She trained and worked on Earth-bound projects at the Kennedy Space Center in Merritt Island, Florida, and the Shuttle Avionics Integration Laboratory in Houston, Texas. Then, on September 28, 1989, Jemison was chosen for a mission to space as part of the STS-47 Spacelab-J seven-person crew.

For the next three years, she prepared for the mission. She studied photography, geology, geography, and the workings of all the systems on the shuttle. She also learned how to fly and scuba dive.

On September 12, 1992, Jemison boarded the *Endeavour* space shuttle as a science mission specialist.

Jemison does a training exercise to prepare for her space mission.

She brought several items with her to represent people who sometimes are not included in events like space travel. One was a statue representing a women's society in West Africa. Another was a flag of Alpha Kappa Alpha, the oldest Black sorority in the US.

Jemison also brought a poster of Judith Jamison, a Black dancer. The poster was a reminder to her that dance and space travel had a connection. "We're very physical beings. So dance is a way of physically exploring the world. So frequently people think of the arts and the sciences as separate and not connected. Both of them are required for creativity. Both of them are required to move the world forward," she said.

GETTING IT DONE!

When Jemison traveled on the *Endeavour*, she became the first Black woman to travel into space.

From left to right, front row: Jerome Apt, Curtis Brown; *back row,* Jan Davis, Mark Lee, Robert Gibson, Jemison, and Mamoru Mohri were members of the STS-47 Spacelab-J crew.

Aboard the *Endeavour*, Jemison worked on two bone cell research experiments. She and the rest of the crew orbited around Earth 126 times. It was an adventure that changed her outlook forever.

Jemison spent 190 hours, thirty minutes, and twenty-three seconds in space. She landed at Kennedy Space Center on September 20, 1992.

"I FELT CONNECTED WITH INFINITY. I FELT CONNECTED WITH THE ENTIRE UNIVERSE WHEN I WAS IN SPACE, AND I FEEL THAT CONNECTION NOW."

Davis (*left*) and Jemison (*right*) did research while working aboard the *Endeavour*.

CHAPTER 4
AFTER NASA

AS AN ASTRONAUT, JEMISON MADE IMPORTANT CONTRIBUTIONS TO SPACE EXPLORATION AND SCIENCE. But she wanted to contribute to the world in new ways. She left NASA in 1993 to start her own companies. The BioSentient Corporation puts her passion for biomedical engineering to work by designing medical equipment. The

Jemison attends the *Star Trek: Nemesis* movie premiere in 2002.

Jemison Group, a technology consulting company, helps bring technology to developing countries.

That year Jemison was invited to play the role of Lieutenant Palmer in an episode of *Star Trek*. She was the first real astronaut to appear on the show.

In 1994 Jemison founded the Dorothy Jemison Foundation for Excellence with her siblings, in memory of their mother. The Earth We Share, an international science camp for students, was started by the foundation. The following year, Jemison began teaching environmental studies at Dartmouth College. She taught there until 2002. During that time, she also wrote *Find Where the Wind Goes: Moments from My Life*, a children's book about her life.

Jemison taught environmental studies at Dartmouth College in New Hampshire.

Jemison presents at a Making Science Make Sense event in 2015.

Jemison started working with Science Matters in 2018. Science Matters encourages kids to get into agricultural science. She wants to make the field of science more diverse. She wants all kids to know that they could study science and help to advance it.

Jemison leads the 100 Year Starship program. It promotes human space travel beyond the solar system within the next century. Jemison is excited about expanding space travel. When she was a child, she imagined astronauts would be able to reach Mars or Jupiter by now. She still wants to help make that kind of trip possible. "You know, when you talk about science, it's very hard for me to tell you as a child, what drew me to it. But I think now as an adult looking back, it was the creativity that drew me to it," she said. "The possibilities."

GETTING IT DONE!

Jemison was inducted into the National Women's Hall of Fame in 1993 and the International Space Hall of Fame in 2004.

YOU'RE THE BOSS

Mae Jemison achieved her goal of traveling in space, even though it didn't always seem possible. She believed in herself and worked hard, but she also had family, friends, and mentors who encouraged and supported her.

Having a support system of your own will help you stay motivated and reach your goals too. Find support by sharing your dreams and goals with others. Pay attention to how they react. Those who encourage you can help you move forward. You may find support from your parents or other family members, as Jemison did. You can also reach out to other adults you trust, like your teachers, school librarian, coach, and principal.

TIMELINE

1956 Mae Carol Jemison is born on October 17 in Decatur, Alabama.

1977 Jemison graduates from Stanford University with degrees in chemical engineering and African American studies.

1981 Jemison graduates from Cornell University with a medical degree.

1987 Jemison is one of fifteen people accepted into NASA's space program.

1992 On September 12, Jemison travels to space aboard the *Endeavour*.

1993 Jemison leaves NASA, founds the Jemison Group, and appears on *Star Trek*.

2004 Jemison is inducted into the International Space Hall of Fame.

2018 Jemison begins work with Science Matters.

GLOSSARY

biomedical engineering: the branch of engineering that builds materials for medicine and health care

consulting: to offer advice or information as an expert of a certain field

engineering: designing and building machines and materials to solve problems

environmental studies: a field of study focused on human interaction with the environment

general practitioner: a medical doctor trained to provide general health care

orbit: the oval or circular path an object takes around another object in space

Peace Corps: an organization that sends volunteers to help people in developing countries

refugee: a person who flees a country to find safety in another country

scholarship: money given to a student for further education

sorority: a club for women at a college

SOURCE NOTES

5 "Mae Jemison: I Wanted to Go into Space," YouTube video, 2:25, posted by Nova's Secret Life of Scientists and Engineers, July 31, 2014, https://www.youtube.com/watch?v=B0vGDfuWhfI.

8 "Dr. Mae C. Jemison," Changing the Face of Medicine, last modified June 3, 2015, https://cfmedicine.nlm.nih.gov/physicians/biography_168.html.

10 "Dr. May Jemison and Defying Gravity: Women in Space," YouTube video, 2:57, posted by Microsoft, October 9, 2018, https://www.youtube.com/watch?v=kkIVhkHsV6I.

13 "Dr. Jemison," Changing the Face of Medicine.

15 "Dr. Jemison."

20 Lauren Wingenroth, "She Was the First Woman of Color in Space—And Dance Helped Her Get There," *Dance Magazine*, July 18, 2019, https://www.dancemagazine.com/mae-jemison-dance-2639198565.html?rebelltitem=1#rebelltitem1.

21 "Girls Ask Dr. Mae Jemison about Space," YouTube video, 1:51, posted by *Good Morning America*, May 23, 2018, https://www.youtube.com/watch?v=JZoDnBoTTxQ.

26 "Dr. Jemison," Changing the Face of Medicine.

LEARN MORE

The Dorothy Jemison Foundation for Excellence: Women of Color in Flight
http://jemisonfoundation.org/women-of-color-in-flight/

Jackson, Libby. *Galaxy Girls: 50 Amazing Stories of Women in Space.* New York: Harper Design, 2018.

Levy, Janey. *Mae Jemison.* New York: Gareth Stevens, 2020.

Moss, Caroline. *Blast Off into Space like May Jemison.* London: Frances Lincoln Children's Books, 2020.

NASA: STEM Engagement
https://www.nasa.gov/stem

National Women's History Museum: Mae Jemison
https://www.womenshistory.org/education-resources/biographies/mae-jemison

National Women's History Museum: Sally Ride
https://www.womenshistory.org/education-resources/biographies/sally-ride

Schwartz, Heather E. *NASA Mathematician Katherine Johnson.* Minneapolis: Lerner Publications, 2018.

INDEX

PHOTO ACKNOWLEDGMENTS

Image credits: NASA, pp. 4, 5, 9, 10, 17, 18, 19, 21, 22; Carol M. Highsmith Archive/Library of Congress (LC-HS503- 2496), p. 6; National Archives of the Netherlands (CC0), p. 7; AP Photo/Mike Fisher, p. 11; BrokenSphere/Wikimedia Commons (CC BY 3.0), p. 12; Linda A. Cicero/Stanford News Service, pp. 13, 14; K-State Research and Extension/flickr (CC BY 2.0), p. 16; AP Photo/Rene Macura, p. 23; Kane5187/Wikimedia Commons (public domain), p. 24; Kevin Wolf/AP Images for Bayer Making Science Make Sense®, p. 25. Design element: kondratya/iStock/Getty Images (handwritten grunge font).

Cover: NASA.